Five reasons why we think you'll love this book!

Winnie AND Wilbur
THE DINOSAUR DAY

This book takes you into a museum and back in time.

Why not be just like Winnie and draw a dinosaur?

There is so much to spot in every picture.

You can take the Winnie and Wilbur challenge: how many stripy legs can you count?

You can join in when Winnie shouts 'Abracadabra!'

Freya

Anushka

Maggie

Bailey

Johannes

Molly

Ashley

Amber

Jun-Yeong

Pablo

Matilda

Marwin

Hasan

Rebecca

Thank you to all these schools for helping with the endpapers:

St Barnabas Primary School, Oxford; St Ebbe's Primary School,
Oxford; Marcham Primary School, Abingdon; St Michael's C.E.
Aided Primary School, Oxford; St Bede's RC Primary School, Jarrow;
The Western Academy, Beijing, China; John King School, Pinxton;
Neston Primary School, Neston; Star of the Sea RC Primary School,
Whitley Bay; José Jorge Letria Primary School, Cascais, Portugal;
Dunmore Primary School, Abingdon; Özel Bahçeşehir İlköğretim
Okulu, Istanbul, Turkey; the International School of Amsterdam, the
Netherlands; Princethorpe Infant School, Birmingham.

For beautiful Cooper—V.T.

For Teddy—K.P.

OXFORD
UNIVERSITY PRESS

Great Clarendon Street, Oxford OX2 6DP

Oxford University Press is a department of the University of
Oxford. It furthers the University's objective of excellence in
research, scholarship,and education by publishing worldwide.
Oxford is a registered trade mark of Oxford University Press in
the UK and in certain other countries

Text copyright © Valerie Thomas 2012
Illustrations copyright © Korky Paul 2012, 2016
The moral rights of the author and artist
have been asserted

Database right Oxford University Press (maker)

First published as *Winnie's Dinosaur Day* in 2012
This edition first published in 2016

British Library Cataloguing in Publication Data available

ISBN: 978-0-19-274819-5 (paperback)
ISBN: 978-0-19-274913-0 (paperback and CD)

10 9 8 7 6 5 4 3 2 1

Printed in China

Paper used in the production of this book is a natural,
recyclable product made from wood grown in
sustainable forests. The manufacturing process
conforms to the environmental regulations of
the country of origin

www.winnieandwilbur.com

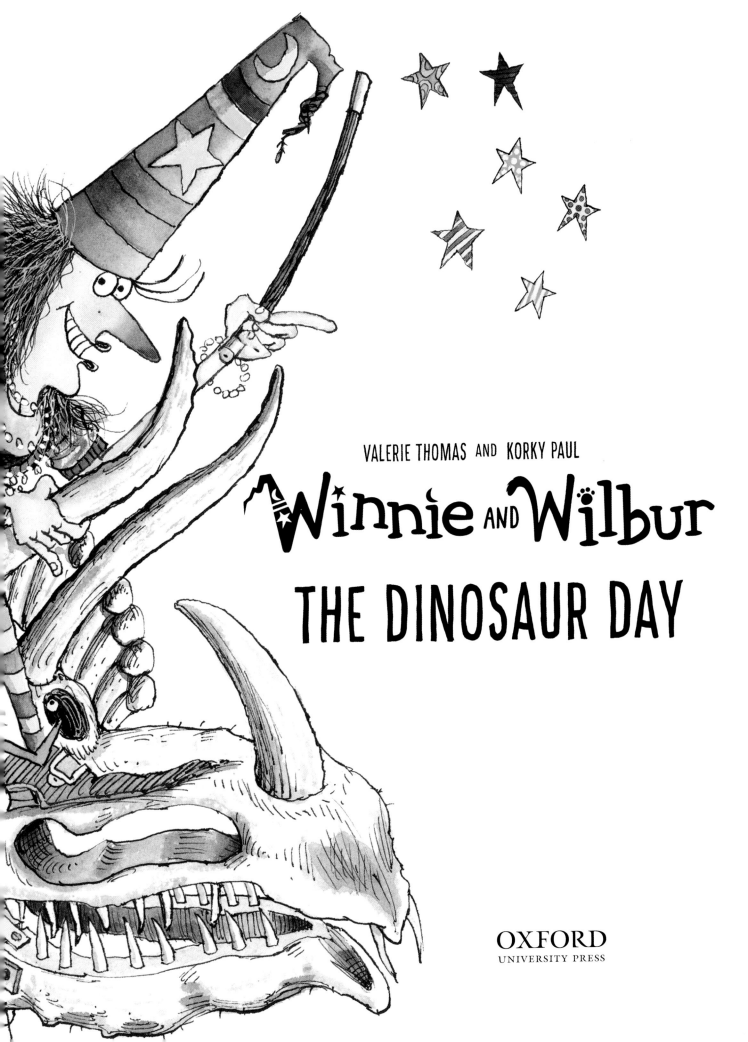

VALERIE THOMAS AND KORKY PAUL

Winnie AND Wilbur

THE DINOSAUR DAY

OXFORD
UNIVERSITY PRESS

Winnie the Witch and her
big black cat Wilbur loved
to visit the museum.

It was full of fascinating things.

There were bugs and beetles and creepy crawlies and slinky snakes.

There were buttons to push, levers to pull, and games to play.

But best of all was the dinosaur room.
Winnie and Wilbur liked to look at
the bones and footprints and models.

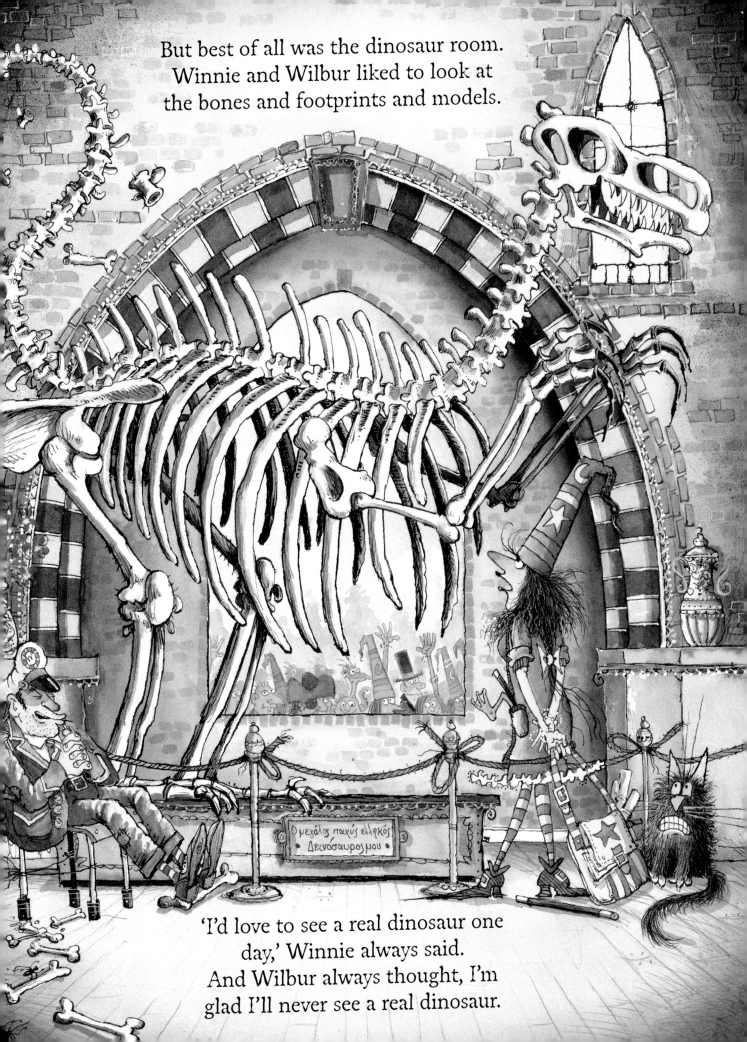

'I'd love to see a real dinosaur one
day,' Winnie always said.
And Wilbur always thought, I'm
glad I'll never see a real dinosaur.

One day, when Winnie and Wilbur
were flying home from the library,
Winnie looked down and saw a big crowd
of people in the museum courtyard.

DINOSAU

'Whatever's happening there?' asked Winnie,
and she flew down to have a look.

There, in the courtyard, was an enormous skeleton.
It was dinosaur week at the museum, and there
was a special competition . . .

WEEK

SPECIAL COMPETITION.
Draw a picture or make a model to show what the **SKELETON** looked like when it was a **DINOSAUR.** AND WIN A PRIZE!

Winnie loved winning prizes.
She looked carefully at the skeleton.
It was very, very big, with lots of spiky bits.

Winnie couldn't decide whether to do a picture or a model, and she couldn't decide what the dinosaur might have looked like.

'It's too hard, Wilbur,' Winnie said. But she really wanted to win the prize.

Then Winnie had an idea.

'Jump on my shoulder, Wilbur,' said Winnie,
and they zoomed up into the sky and back
to Winnie's house.

Winnie got out her
Big Book of Spells.
'Yes!' she said.

She shut her eyes,
stamped her foot
and shouted,

'Abracadabra!'

There was a flash of fire,
a great WHOOOSH . . .

and Winnie and Wilbur were back in the time of the dinosaurs.

There were dinosaurs everywhere.
Big dinosaurs, enormous dinosaurs,
gigantic dinosaurs!

Winnie and Wilbur hid in a tree.

'Now all we have to do is find a dinosaur
that looks like the skeleton,' said Winnie.
'That should be easy.'
'Meeow,' said Wilbur.
He didn't like the time of the dinosaurs.

Winnie looked around carefully.
'There it is!' she shouted.
'Of course. It's a triceratops.
Look at its three horns, Wilbur.'
'Meeeoow!' said Wilbur.

He didn't want to look.
He wanted to go home.

Winnie got out her drawing book
and her coloured pencils.
It was much easier drawing a *real* dinosaur.

Her drawing looked *exactly* like the triceratops.
Well, it looked quite like the triceratops.

'This is an excellent drawing,' said Winnie.
'It's sure to win the prize.

But now we need to get back to the museum.
I know! The triceratops can take us.'
'Meeeoow!' said Wilbur.
He put his paws over his eyes.

Winnie picked him up, jumped onto the dinosaur's
back, waved her magic wand and shouted,

'Abracadabra!'

. . . and the dinosaur **WHOOSHED** off to the museum.

Professor Perkins was getting ready to present the prize when the dinosaur landed in the courtyard.

Everybody was very surprised!

'Well,' said Professor Perkins, 'I think we all know who has won the competition.'

And he gave a big shiny medal
to the triceratops.
The dinosaur was delighted.
He had never won a prize before.

Winnie didn't mind too much.

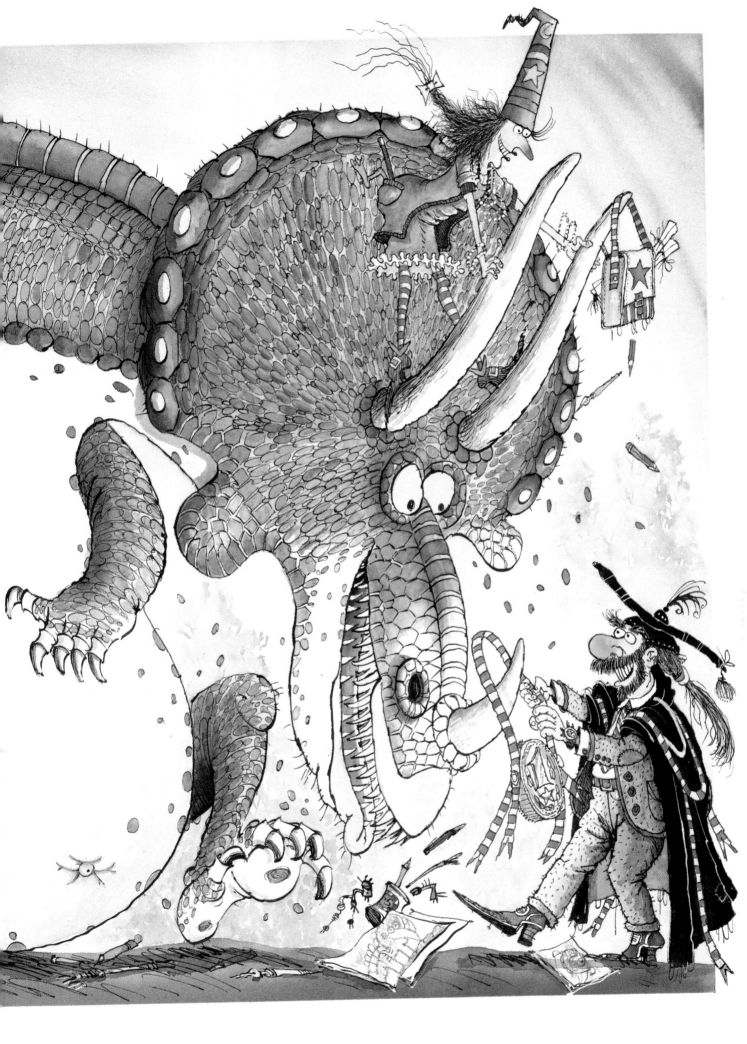

Then Winnie and Wilbur took the
dinosaur home for tea.

The dinosaur didn't like sandwiches
or muffins or cakes.

But he enjoyed eating Winnie's trees
and her roses were delicious.

'Oh dear,' Winnie said. 'He'll eat
my whole garden! It's a pity he's so big,
Wilbur. He's such a nice dinosaur.'

Then Winnie had a wonderful idea.
She waved her magic wand, shouted,

'Abracadabra!'

and the **enormous** dinosaur was a tiny dinosaur.

So now Winnie never has to cut her grass.
And Wilbur has a playmate that is just the right size!

Bethany

Katia

Eun-Jae

Kathleen

Ji-Eun

Jenny

Sara

Fraser

Ka Keung

Selin

Selin

Olivia

Siyabend

Kieran

A note for grown-ups

Oxford Owl is a FREE and easy-to-use website packed with support and advice about everything to do with reading.

Informative videos

Hints, tips and fun activities

Top tips from top writers for reading with your child

Help with choosing picture books

For this expert advice and much, much more about how children learn to read and how to keep them reading ...

LOOK
for Oxford Owl
www.oxfordowl.co.uk